For Mom & Dad, from your
loving daughter Colleen Waring ~ C.M.

Published for Scholastic Inc., 557 Broadway, New York, NY 10012,
by arrangement with Little Tiger Press.
SCHOLASTIC and associated logos are trademarks and/or
registered trademarks of Scholastic Inc.
Scholastic Canada Ltd.; Markham, Ontario

Original edition published in English by Little Tiger Press,
an imprint of Magi Publications, London, England, 2008

Text and Illustrations copyright © Colleen McKeown 2008

ISBN-10: 1-84506-943-9; ISBN-13: 978-1-84506-943-8

Printed in China

1 3 5 7 9 10 8 6 4 2

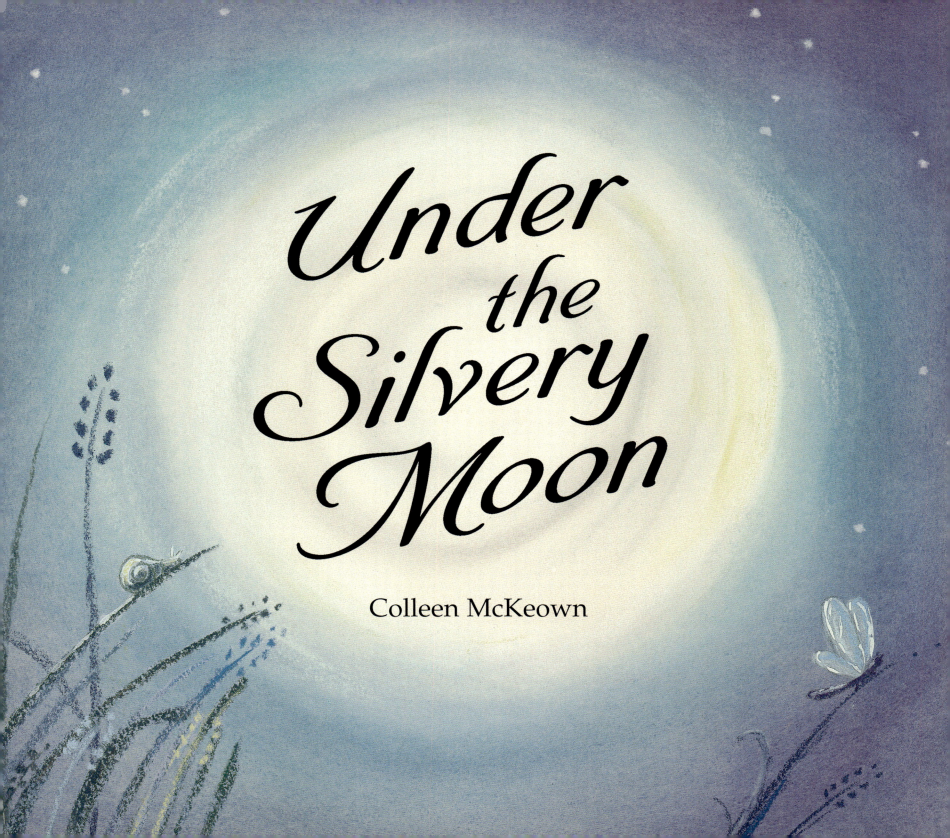

Under the Silvery Moon

Colleen McKeown

The stars were shining brightly.
Little Kitten was in bed.
But up he sat, still wide awake.
"Sleep now," his mother said.

"But it's so noisy, I can't sleep!"
said Kitten with a sigh.
"It's just our friends," said Mother Cat.
"They're waking up nearby . . . .

"The tiny mice are playing;
  they explore the barn at night.
They skip and scamper here and there
  beneath the warm lamplight.

"Hush, Kitten, can you hear it,
that shuffling, snuffling sound?
The hedgehogs look for food to eat
along the moonlit ground.

"That cry you hear, so long and loud,
that distant, haunting tune,
Belongs to fox, who's up at night.
He's calling to the Moon.

"Around us swirls a summer song;
    it's whispered through the trees.
The evening wind is blowing
    through the softly rustling leaves.

"Beyond the midnight meadow,
    where the air is soft and cool,
The frogs are gently croaking
    all around the moonlit pool.

"Some creatures are not stirring;
they do not make a peep.
Like us, they've had a busy day,
and now they're fast asleep.

"The badgers stretch their sturdy legs
and blink into the dark.
'Good evening,' they are calling,
with a deep and playful bark.

"The nimble hares are dancing;
their paws thump on the ground.
With joyful leaps they chase their tails
and spring and dart around.

"Something quiet and gentle
 lights up the dark night skies.
Glowing warm and lovely
 are the dreamy fireflies.

"Owl is hooting softly;
 across the stars she glides.
Soaring home toward the barn,
 upon the wind she rides.

"And so you see, my little one,
    there's nothing you should fear.
Our friends' nighttime adventures
    are all that you can hear."

Little Kitten closed his eyes
    and hugged his mother tight.
"It's time you went to sleep," she purred.
    "Sweet dreams, my love, good night."